The Drugstore Cat

Beacon Press Night Lights

Lonesome Boy
Arna Bontemps
Illustrated by Feliks Topolski

Where Is Daddy? The Story of a Divorce
Beth Goff
Illustrated by Susan Perl

The Drugstore Cat

ANN PETRY

Illustrated by Susanne Suba

BEACON PRESS   BOSTON

Beacon Press
25 Beacon Street
Boston, Massachusetts 02108

Beacon Press books
are published under the auspices of
the Unitarian Universalist Association of Congregations.

© 1949 by Ann Petry
First published as a Beacon Night Light in 1988
All rights reserved
Printed in the United States of America
95 94 93 92 91 90 89 88   8 7 6 5 4 3 2 1

Library of Congress Cataloging-in-Publication Data
Petry, Ann Lane, 1911–
    The drugstore cat / Ann Petry; illustrated by Susanne Suba.
    p.   cm.
    Summary: A little cat with a short temper tries to learn the
difficult lesson of patience and self-restraint.
    ISBN 0-8070-8308-9
    ISBN 0-8070-8309-7 (pbk.)
    [1. Cats—Fiction.]   I. Suba, Susanne, 1913–   ill.   II. Title.
PZ7.P4473Dr 1988   88-3308

This book is for
ANNA HOUSTON BUSH
and
ANNA LOUISE JAMES

Contents

CHAPTER ONE

Buzzie Goes to His New Home

Buzzie was a round, fat kitten. His fur was gray with touches of yellow under his chin and on his paws. He was just the color of smoke as it comes up from a pile of burning leaves.

He had a very short tail and a very loud purr. When he was happy he purred so loudly that he sounded exactly like a small warm motor—buzz-zz, buzz-zz, buzz-zz. That is why he was called Buzzie.

His first home was in a big red barn. He lived there with his mother and his three brothers and two sisters.

One morning his mother washed him, all over, very carefully, while she told him that he was going to have a new home; and that he was to go to his new home that night.

"It's in a drugstore, Buzzie," his mother said. "And you must mind your manners so that Miss James and her brother, Mr. James, will like you. It's a very good place to live."

Buzzie got so excited at the thought of going somewhere brand new that he skipped away from his mother before she finished washing his face. He ran over to his brothers and sisters to tell them that he was going away.

"I never did think much of this as a place to live," Buzzie said, staring at the wisps of hay on the barn floor. "I'm going to live in a drugstore. I bet you wish *you* were," he said to the other kittens.

He could tell by the way they tumbled against

him, and by the questions they asked, that they wanted to go away with him. He never once thought that he might miss his mother and these brothers and sisters after he reached his new home. But he did wonder how he would get back to the barn if he decided he didn't want to stay at the drugstore.

So he ran back to his mother. "What will I do if I don't like living in a drugstore?" he asked.

His mother half closed her eyes and looked very wise. She began washing his right ear. He tried to wriggle away from her. But she held him firmly with one paw.

"Oh, you'll like the drugstore," she said. "Of course you won't have anyone to talk to," her tongue moved down the side of his face. "But you'll get used to that."

"Why won't I have anyone to talk to?" Buzzie asked, alarmed. He drew closer to his mother although her tongue was very rough. She washed a little harder around his right ear and he drew back.

"Because, my dear, human beings can't understand what cats say. You will be able to understand what they say. But they won't understand you."

"That's very queer," Buzzie said. "How will the people I'm going to live with know my name if they can't understand what I say?" he asked anxiously.

"Anyone who hears you purr will know that your name should be 'Buzzie.' And Miss James and her brother, Mr. James, who own the drugstore, are very bright people. They'll know your name once you purr very loudly for them."

"Why don't humans understand what cats say?" Buzzie asked.

"They just don't," his mother said flatly and changed the subject. "Now you remember that your father was a Manx cat—"

"What's a Manx cat?" Buzzie said, not waiting for her to finish what she was saying.

His mother sighed and gave him a gentle push, to remind him that he wasn't minding his manners.

"A Manx cat," she said, "is a cat with a short tail like yours. You look very much like your father. He was a fine cat. And I expect you to make him proud of you."

Buzzie tried to peer around at his tail while his mother washed his neck. It was hard to do but he finally caught a glimpse of his tail. Then he looked at his brothers and sisters. Their tails were long. His tail was really very short.

He looked at his mother's tail. It was long and slender. As he looked at it she moved it gracefully.

"I want a long tail, too," he wailed.

"That's a very smart length tail you have," his mother said firmly. "There are very few cats with elegant short tails like that. Now you go to sleep so you'll be rested when Mr. James comes for you."

When Mr. James came to get Buzzie, it was dark outside. Buzzie's mother and his brothers and sisters stood in the barn door, watching, as Mr. James carried Buzzie out to his car.

The last thing Buzzie heard his mother say was, "Now remember! I've never had a kitten sent back to me. So you mind your manners!"

5

In the car, Buzzie purred very softly, to show Mr. James that he wanted to be friendly. Then he said, "My name is Buzzie."

Mr. James did not answer. Buzzie stopped purring and sat up straight in Mr. James's lap. "I wish I had someone to talk to," he said to himself.

The swaying motion of the car made him dizzy. The smell of gasoline got in his nose and he sneezed. It seemed to Buzzie that they rode for miles and miles, though they really didn't.

Finally the car stopped in front of the drugstore. The drugstore was in a building that was painted red. Lights shone out through the big glass window. Though Buzzie couldn't read it there was a big sign across the front of the building that said 'James Drugstore' in shiny letters.

Mr. James carried Buzzie up the store steps so fast that Buzzie did not see the tall elm trees that lined the street, or a church across the way, with a white steeple that went up and up.

Mr. James walked straight through the drugstore,

6

carrying Buzzie. When he reached a little room in the back, he put the kitten on the floor.

There were rows and rows of bottles on the shelves. At one end of the little room there was a long high counter with a stool in front of it.

Buzzie walked all around the little room, sniffing at the bottles on the floor. Then a woman with gray hair came out of the drugstore and stood looking down at Buzzie over the top of her glasses. This was Miss James, Mr. James's sister.

"I wonder if *she* can understand me when I talk," Buzzie said under his breath. Then in his very best speaking voice he said, "I guess you must be Miss James. I'm your new cat." He looked up at her hopefully.

Miss James did not answer. Buzzie knew then that his mother had been right. Neither Mr. James nor Miss James could understand a word he said.

Miss James looked at her brother and said, "Why, that little cat has hardly any tail!"

Buzzie looked around at his short tail. It was really

8

very short. His mother's tail was a beautiful length. But his mother had told him that this was a very smart length tail that he had.

He held his short tail straight up in order to make it look longer. Then he started walking in and out, in and out, between Mr. James's long legs.

"I don't think I'm going to like living in a drugstore," he said out loud, to himself. After all he had to have someone to talk to. "Miss James doesn't like my tail. And I haven't anyone to talk to."

He began thinking about the barn. His brothers and sisters would be lying in the sweet-smelling hay, curled up next to their mother. And right now she would be telling them stories, and purring songs to them. Oh, how he wished he was with them!

"Meow," he said, very sadly.

Miss James looked down at him, over the top of her glasses. "He's got a very big voice for such a little cat," she said. Her eyebrows went up very high.

Someone came in the drugstore and Miss James went out of the little backroom.

"I'm going to bed," Mr. James said. He leaned over and rubbed the top of Buzzie's small head. Then Mr. James went out of the little room, too.

Buzzie followed right behind Mr. James. They went up a long flight of stairs. When they reached the second floor, Buzzie walked away from Mr. James. He peered in the bedroom, stuck his paw inside a closet door, and then wandered out into a hall. He found another flight of stairs and went down them.

There was a dining room and a kitchen downstairs. He paused in front of the ice box in the kitchen and sniffed.

"I bet there's meat in there," he said to himself.

He poked his head through the living room door. The chairs looked soft, as though they might be good places to take a nap in.

"It's a little lonely over here," he said. "Guess I'll go back to the drugstore side."

He went up the stairs, through the hall, and came down the stairs on the other side of the building.

Miss James was sitting in a chair by the window in the little back room.

Buzzie walked over to where she was sitting and looked up at her. "I suppose I have to try to make her want to keep me in spite of my short tail. My mother told me this was a good place to live," he said thoughtfully.

He held up one of his front paws. His feet were cold, for there was a draft coming from the stairs. Miss James's lap ought to be soft and warm.

Up he jumped and landed in the middle of her lap.

"Meow," he said, softly. Then he started to purr, for her lap was very soft and very warm. His purring grew louder and louder as his feet got warmer and warmer. He said, "Buzz-zz, buzz-zz, buzz-zz."

Miss James stroked his small gray head. "You seem to be a friendly little buzzie cat," she said gently. "A buzzie cat," she repeated. "Why I think we'll call you Buzzie. You're a friendly little cat."

"I like you, too," Buzzie said.

He waited patiently for an answer. But Miss James did not say anything.

CHAPTER TWO

Buzzie Finds a Friend

When Buzzie woke up the next morning, he arched his back. And stretched each of his legs, way out. He blinked his eyes. Open and shut. Open and shut. Open and shut.

He opened his mouth wide and yawned and showed his pink curved tongue. With his mouth open he looked as though he were laughing. His stiff white whiskers moved up toward his ears, and the

13

corners of his mouth turned up that way, too.

He thought he was in his home, in the barn, with his brothers and sisters and his mother. So he said, very softly, "I guess I'll go back to sleep for a few minutes. The others aren't awake yet. And it's a little lonesome to be awake all by myself."

He closed his eyes, tightly. Then he reached out a paw to touch his mother. He wanted to let her know that he was not asleep even though his eyes were closed.

His mother was not there!

Buzzie opened his eyes, jumped up, and looked around. He was very much surprised when he found that he was not in the barn. Then he remembered that he was in his new home. He had been sleeping on a red cushion on the floor of Miss James's kitchen.

"Why!" he said. "I'm all by myself! My mother isn't here to tell me to wash my face and mind my manners. And I don't have anyone to talk to or to play with."

When Miss James came into the kitchen, Buzzie

was sitting up very straight, in the middle of the floor.

He said, "Meow!" very softly when he saw her. He was wondering what he was going to do all day without his brothers and sisters to play Hunt and Cat-and-Mouse with him.

Miss James warmed some milk and poured it into a blue bowl. She put the bowl down on the floor near Buzzie.

He lapped the milk up, quickly. "My! But I was hungry," he said to Miss James. While he licked the bowl clean, he kept turning his head to see if she was going to answer him. But she did not say anything.

After he finished his breakfast he washed himself, all over, very carefully. Then Miss James opened the kitchen door.

Buzzie went outside and sat down on the kitchen steps. His nose twitched as he smelt the fresh morning air. Once he glanced up at the sun. He blinked his eyes and stared at the backyard.

The grass was green and smooth. In the center of

the lawn there was a bird bath. Three robins were taking their morning bath in it, splashing water and talking to themselves.

"I wonder if I could catch one of those robins if I walked very quickly, very very quickly, and very softly, very very softly, down the middle of the lawn," Buzzie said.

He moved so quickly that before you knew it he was halfway down the yard. His feet stayed close to the ground and his short fat body was touching the grass.

Suddenly the robins flew up out of the bird bath.

"Oh, drumsticks!" Buzzie said. "They must have seen me."

He lay down in the grass. "I can't even sneak up on a bird," he said. "And my mother isn't here to tell me where I made a mistake."

He was very angry. He blinked his eyes and his short tail flicked back and forth, back and forth. So he said, "Drumsticks! Drumsticks!" twice, like that. Then he felt a little better.

He rolled over in the soft, cool grass. While he was lying on his back he looked up at the sky. It was like a high blue roof over his head. Then he turned over on his stomach and looked around the yard.

On one side there were small evergreen trees. And on the other side of the yard there were rambler roses growing along a white picket fence. Buzzie got up and walked toward the fence.

"Under those bushes would be a fine place for a young cat like me to take afternoon naps," he said. "No one would see me and it would be cool there on a warm day."

He lifted his feet high as he walked across the lawn. Now and then a blade of grass tickled the bottom of his feet.

All of a sudden he heard someone say, "Hello, Cat!"

Buzzie stood still. He stared at the picket fence, at the scarlet roses, at the small evergreen trees, but he couldn't see who it was that had spoken.

"You can't see me, Cat. But I can see you," said the voice.

Buzzie looked back over his shoulder, then up at the sky that was like a blue roof, high over his head, and he still couldn't see who had spoken. "Who wants to see you anyway?" he said, sharply.

Then he jumped straight up in the air. For the voice said, "Lots of people want to see me."

Buzzie began to breathe very fast. "Why, it's a

human being," he said softly. "And he can understand me when I talk. I wish my mother were here.
Maybe she could explain this."

He walked closer to the picket fence. There,
crouched down on the other side of the fence, was a
small boy. The boy had on short blue pants and a
white shirt. He had very large eyes for such a small
fellow and he was looking straight at Buzzie.

When the boy saw that Buzzie had found him and
was looking at him, he said, "Hello, Cat," again and
smiled.

"Hello, yourself," said Buzzie. And then he said,
"Say, what's your name?"

The little boy said, "My name is Peter. What's
your name, Cat?"

Buzzie held his short tail up very straight and
began to purr. Then he said, "My mother told me
anybody who heard me purr would know that my
name is Buzzie. So don't call me 'Cat' or I'll call you
'Boy.' "

When Buzzie said this he tried to make his voice

sound big and angry. But he really wasn't angry. He was pleased because he had found someone he could talk to.

"I live over there," Peter said, pointing to a large house on the other side of the picket fence. The house was painted white. It had dark green shutters. There was a wide driveway near the house.

"I live at the drugstore with Miss James and her brother, Mr. James," Buzzie said. He rubbed against the picket fence and purred, louder and louder. He was so happy to have someone to talk to.

"Does Miss James sleep in the drugstore?" Peter asked.

"Of course not," Buzzie said. "The drugstore is one half of the downstairs part on the other side of the house and she sleeps upstairs. The kitchen and the dining room are the other half of the downstairs part on this side."

After saying so many words at once Buzzie had to stop and take a deep breath. You see he was so pleased to find someone who understood what he said that he hadn't been able to stop talking long enough to take a breath in between the words.

He looked at Peter out of the corner of his eyes. "How do you understand what I say?" he asked.

"Well, you're talking and I can hear, can't I?" Peter looked surprised.

Buzzie wanted to tell him that that wasn't a very good answer. Miss James and her brother could hear, too, but they could not understand what a cat said.

But he didn't get time to say this. Someone inside Peter's house called out, "Peter! Come and eat your breakfast."

"Yes'm," Peter said. "Come on, Buzzie."

"Oh, no!" Buzzie said. "I've already had my breakfast."

"Well, you can watch me eat." And before Buzzie could walk away, Peter reached through the picket fence and picked him up. Then he pulled Buzzie through one of the openings in the fence.

Peter held Buzzie very tightly as he walked toward the back door of the big white house.

"Don't hold me so tight," Buzzie said, squirming.

"I'm sorry," Peter said. "But I was afraid you'd run back home."

Buzzie tried to twist himself out of Peter's arms and he did not stop twisting and turning until Peter's mother came to the door.

Peter's mother said, "Oh, there you are!" and smiled. She had on a pink apron. And in her black curly hair she wore a ribbon which was the same pink color as the apron. She frowned when she saw Peter holding Buzzie in his arms.

"Where did you get that little cat?" she said. "Put him down this very minute. Now you'll have to wash your face and hands all over again before you can eat your breakfast."

Peter put Buzzie down in the wide driveway. Buzzie began to pace up and down, up and down. His short tail moved back and forth as he walked.

Peter's mother looked at Buzzie and laughed. "Why, I do believe he's angry," she said. And then she laughed so hard she very nearly cried. "Oh,

look!" she said. "That little cat doesn't have any tail!"

"What's the matter with her?" Buzzie asked Peter. "First of all I washed myself, all over, this morning. I'm just as clean as I can be. And, second of all, I do so have a tail. It's very short, I know, but it's a smart length tail."

Peter's mother went right on laughing. And Buzzie said, "I'm going home."

Peter called to him. "Buzzie! Buzzie! Don't go."

But Buzzie did not answer. He ran across the wide driveway, slipped under the picket fence, and then ran quickly across Miss James's lawn. When he reached the kitchen steps he sat down, breathing hard.

After he caught his breath he began to talk to himself.

"I wish I were back in the barn," he said. "I wish, I wish, I wish, OH, how I wish I were back in the barn!"

Then he said, "DRUMSTICKS!" And he began to feel a little better.

CHAPTER THREE

Buzzie Goes for a Walk

While Buzzie sat on the kitchen steps he washed his right paw and cleaned his whiskers. He looked very thoughtful. He wished he hadn't lost his temper.

"Oh, drumsticks!" he said, softly, under his breath.

He gave his whiskers a final polish and then lay down on the top step. Stretching out full length, he looked at the big backyard.

It was a shining day. The sun made the grass and the small evergreen trees glow. Even the leaves of the ivy, growing on the kitchen chimney close by, gleamed in the sunlight. The air was sweet with the smell of honeysuckle and of roses.

"Now what am I going to do all day, here by myself?" he said. Suddenly he sat up. "I'll go for a walk! This is a fine morning to see what the town looks like."

As soon as he said this he ran down the kitchen steps. He paused once to swat at a fly that passed within an inch of his nose. The fly darted away as though it, too, had some special business on this shining morning.

Buzzie slipped through the picket fence and walked across the grass. There was a dirt path in front of the drugstore. He trotted briskly down the path, going away from the store, hurrying along as though he knew exactly where he was going. He really didn't. He was only going for a walk. Now and then he paused to poke at a pebble, or to sniff at the grass which grew fresh and green on each side of the path.

He hadn't gone very far when he suddenly stood still. Then he sat down, right in the middle of the path, to get a better look at a very very old man who was walking toward him.

The old man wore a wide-brimmed panama hat and in his hand he carried a gold-headed cane. He was walking with a quick light step and as he walked he twirled the cane in front of him.

The gold head on the cane was so shiny that it looked as though a small sun were moving up and down, and back and forth, in front of the old gentleman.

Buzzie blinked his eyes as the man came nearer. For the sunlight gleamed on the gold head on the cane. And the panama hat looked as though it were transparent.

The old gentleman smiled when he saw Buzzie sitting in the middle of the path. He stopped and spoke to him.

"Good morning, sir!" he said, in a deep friendly

voice. He leaned over and patted the top of Buzzie's head. "This is a fine morning for a walk."

"It certainly is," Buzzie said. He got up and walked in between the man's long legs, in and out, in and out. And all the time he kept one eye on the gold-headed cane. "I thought I'd find out where this path leads to."

"You must be a stranger here," the old man said.

"Yes," said Buzzie. "I'm Miss James's new cat. I live at the drugstore. I purr very loudly. That's why my name is Buzzie." After he said this, he purred very loudly to show how he got his name. He sounded exactly like a small, warm motor–buzz-zz, buzz-zz, buzz-zz.

The old gentleman straightened up, lifted his wide-brimmed hat and bowed. "I'm delighted to meet you, Buzzie. I'm Mr. Smith."

When Mr. Smith said this he twirled his cane. Buzzie stopped walking in and out between Mr. Smith's legs and stared straight at the cane with both eyes. He found that he was blinking again. For the

gold head on the cane shone like the sun itself. And looking at it was just like looking straight at a very small and shiny sun.

Mr. Smith lifted the panama hat and bowed again.

"Well, I hope you will meet with a Pleasant Adventure on your walk. Good day to you, sir," he said in his deep friendly voice.

"Good day, yourself, Mr. Smith," Buzzie said.

Then Buzzie went trotting down the path, lifting his feet high, and holding his short tail straight up in the air.

Suddenly he stood still. Then he gave a little jump. He turned his head and looked back at Mr. Smith.

"Why, he understood me when I talked!" said Buzzie. "That's very queer. I wonder if my mother was wrong. I've found two people who understand cat language—Peter and Mr. Smith."

Buzzie went on down the path, and as he trotted along, he made up a small song, just for the fun of it. He said, "That makes two of them. Two of them. Two of them that understand me."

30

He began to take little running steps. Once he stopped to chase his short tail, around and around, and under his breath he kept saying, "Two of them, two of them, two of them, two of them, that understand me."

He paused for a moment under a big elm tree. For somewhere high up in the branches, over his head, a bird twittered. He looked up at the bird.

"Oh, go away, Mrs. Robin," he said. "I'm not going to bother your children."

Just beyond the big elm tree, the path ended. A wide black road went straight ahead, and curving off to the right was another narrower road.

"I guess I'll find out where that wide road goes," Buzzie said to himself.

He started across the road. He looked very small because the road was so wide. He kept turning his head to see if there were any cars coming.

He forgot to watch the road that curved off to the right. He was halfway across when a long shiny black car swooped out from the side road.

Buzzie did not see the car. He heard it. The sound of the motor roared in his ears. He ran so fast his short fat body almost touched the ground. His heart pounded against his ribs. He felt a hot blast of air against his fur.

Then he was across the road. He did not stop running until he reached the path that bordered the road. He was trembling and his breath was coming so hard and so fast that his small sides were heaving. He had to sit down in the middle of the path to catch his breath.

The long shiny car stopped and then slid slowly backward. It stopped again, in front of Buzzie.

The young man who was driving the car leaned out. "Why don't you look where you're going?" he said. "I almost ran over you."

Buzzie got to his feet. His legs were shaking. He was still breathing very hard.

"Why don't you look where YOU'RE going?" he asked angrily. "A cat certainly has a right to cross the street."

The young man grinned. "You certainly are a short-tempered little cat!" he said. "I can't understand a word you're saying but I know you're being very rude from those hissing sounds you're making."

"Drumsticks!" Buzzie exclaimed. His voice shook and that made him still angrier. So he said, "DRUMSTICKS!" again, in his very loudest voice. His voice still shook, but he began to feel better.

"I've got to lie down," he said. "I'm awfully tired. That gasoline smell is still in my nose." His nostrils twitched as he tried to get the fresh-air smell back.

The grass that edged the path was very high. Buzzie left the path, "I'll lie down in here," he said. As he walked through the high grass, it parted in front of him as though it were bowing to him.

He had not gone very far when he came upon a big flat stone. He lifted his head. A quick gathering of his muscles and he jumped up. The stone was warm from the sun. He walked all around the edge of it. Then he curled up in the middle of the stone and went to sleep.

CHAPTER FOUR

Buzzie Stays Out All Night

When Buzzie woke up he lay perfectly still on top of the big flat stone. He watched the high grass sway back and forth, back and forth, as a gentle breeze blew through it.

The sun was warm on his fur. He stretched out full length and yawned, showing his white pointed teeth and his cupped pink tongue. Then he sat up and sniffed the air. He caught the odor of field mice.

34

He stared very hard at the tall grass in the meadow.

"Why, I'm hungry," he said. "I ought to be going home to eat my lunch."

He jumped down from the big flat stone. The grass was high over his head. It rustled in the breeze. He sniffed the air again. It smelt ever so faintly of field mice.

"I'm not going home to eat," he said. "I'll hunt for a mouse. And eat it right here in the meadow."

Buzzie walked farther and farther into the meadow. The ground was damp under his feet. The smell of field mice grew stronger.

He crouched close to the ground, moving slowly, and so quietly that the long grass barely moved as he crept through it. This was the way his mother had taught him to hunt.

"I bet my mother would be proud of me if she could see me," he thought.

Suddenly he stopped creeping through the grass and poked at a beetle which was scurrying along the damp ground. The beetle ran under a rusted tin can.

35

Buzzie poked at the can with his paw. He forgot about the beetle and the field mice.

The can was round. It rolled whenever he touched it. He began to play with it, jumping over it, and then lying still, and suddenly pushing it along in front of him with his paw.

He found an opening in the top of the can and sniffed at it. There was a strong, fishy smell inside. He pushed his right paw in through the opening, forcing it in. The opening was small. It took him quite a while to get his paw inside the can.

The fish smell was so strong and so tempting that he kept forcing his paw farther and farther inside, trying to reach the bottom of the can.

He pushed in his paw just as far as it would go. No matter how hard he pushed, he could not touch the bottom of the can.

"Drumsticks!" he said, angrily.

He tried to pull his paw out of the can. The sharp ragged edge, which had been bent inward, cut him.

He kept turning and twisting. No matter which

36

way he moved he was not able to pull his paw out of the can!

"Oh, DRUMSTICKS!" he said, twice. He gave his paw a hard, angry jerk. The pain made him cry out.

He lay still for a moment. Then he began walking, on three legs. The can cut his paw with each step. He found that it was easier to walk backward and drag the can behind him as he went. He backed into an old tree stump and after that he lay still.

While he lay there in the long grass it grew dark. The stars came out. He heard a dog trot up the road, heard the jingle-jangle of the tag against the dog's collar. But before he heard these sounds, his nostrils dilated from the dog smell. Fear made his ears flatten against his head.

The dog smell grew stronger and Buzzie held his breath. Then a skunk pattered up the road, pausing now and then to sniff. The dog barked and started chasing the skunk.

The air was suddenly full of a choking, bitter

37

smell. The dog yelped and ran up the road. The jingle-jangle of the tags grew fainter and finally the sound disappeared entirely.

"I wonder if the skunk could tell me what to do if I called out to him," Buzzie said.

But the smell of the skunk was so strong and so bitter that Buzzie kept quiet.

Buzzie Stays Out All Night

His paw ached. He could not go to sleep. At first he wished he was back in the barn with his mother and his brothers and sisters. Then he wished he was in the drugstore, and then, that he was anywhere but alone here in the wide meadow.

As the night wore on, he heard all the sounds of the night, the rustling of the grass, the murmuring of the wind, the whirring sound made by the wings of some night-flying bird. Somewhere in the distance an owl hooted and a small bird chirped sleepily.

Toward dawn, the wind shifted. The air grew warmer. Long streaks of light came into the sky.

Buzzie got up and started walking, slowly, painfully, on his three good legs. His paw ached so that he could walk only a few steps before he had to rest. Walk and then rest. Walk and then rest.

The sun came up. It looked like a half-closed eye, a brilliant yellow eye, peering over the edge of the meadow. Buzzie stopped to get his breath. When he began his slow, painful walk again, the sun was all the way up.

It was a long time before he reached the path. He lay down near the edge of it.

"I'll take a nap right here," he said. "I ache so."

He had been asleep only a little while when the sound of footsteps woke him up. He looked behind him. Mr. Smith was walking briskly up the path, swinging his gold-headed cane in front of him.

"Meow," said Buzzie, in a voice so small that it was almost like the sound of the wind whispering through the tall grass.

Then he took a deep breath. "Mr. Smith! Mr. Smith!" he said in his very loudest voice.

Mr. Smith looked all around, up at the blue sky, down at the tall grass in the meadow, and, finally, down at the path. When he saw Buzzie, lying there with his paw held fast in the rusted can, he said, "Hello, there! It's my new friend." And then, "Well, well, well, Sir! This isn't a very Pleasant Adventure."

"My leg hurts so," Buzzie said.

"Of course it does," said Mr. Smith. He leaned

over and laid his gold-headed cane down on the path, right in front of Buzzie.

"Now you lie quite still," Mr. Smith said gently. "And I'll get your paw out of that can in the shake of a lamb's tail. Yes, sir, in the shake of a lamb's tail! And that's no time at all."

Mr. Smith took a pen knife out of his vest pocket. He said, "Now you look at that gold head on my cane. Then you take a deep breath, and open and shut your eyes three times. And I'll have your paw out of that can before a lamb could give a good shake to his tail."

Buzzie looked straight at the gold head on the cane, just as Mr. Smith had told him to do. It was like looking at a very small sun. Then he took a deep breath and opened and shut his eyes three times. He thought the gold head on the cane winked at him but it was only because he had opened and shut his eyes so fast.

Mr. Smith patted Buzzie's head and said, "One!"

Then he pried a bigger opening in the can with

41

his sharp little pen knife. And said, "Two!"

Buzzie jumped from the sudden, sharp pain in his paw. He hissed angrily. His short tail started going back and forth, back and forth. He was just about to scratch Mr. Smith. Then he lay still. He was ashamed to have been angry when Mr. Smith was trying so hard to help him.

Mr. Smith pulled Buzzie's paw very gently but very firmly out of the can and said, "That makes Three! And a lamb couldn't possibly shake his tail in that length of time."

Buzzie moved his paw. He was so pleased to find that it was free of the can that he began to purr, even though the paw ached.

"I'll carry you up to the drugstore," Mr. Smith said and picked Buzzie up. "Miss James will fix your paw so that it'll be just as good as new in a few weeks."

Buzzie was so comfortable in Mr. Smith's arms that he purred all the way up the street. He kept blinking his eyes at the gold-headed cane.

"How do you know so much about cats?" Buzzie asked.

Mr. Smith patted Buzzie's small head. "When a man gets to be as old as I am there isn't much he doesn't know about cats and dogs and boys and girls."

When Mr. Smith came in the store carrying Buzzie, Miss James was very upset.

"I can't imagine what made him run away!" Miss James said. "We looked *everywhere* and couldn't find him."

Mr. Smith said, "Oh, he just went for a walk."
And as he went out of the store he waved his cane at
Buzzie.

Miss James washed Buzzie's hurt paw and bandaged it. And all the time she kept saying, "I don't
know why you ran away."

Buzzie said, "But I didn't run away. I went for a
walk. And then I went in the meadow to catch a
mouse. And my paw got stuck in a tin can. I really
didn't run away."

But Miss James could not understand a word he
said.

CHAPTER FIVE

Buzzie Scratches a Customer

For the next three days, Buzzie spent most of the time sleeping on the red cushion in Miss James's kitchen. He woke up, and ate, and then went back to sleep. And woke up, and ate, and went back to sleep.

On the afternoon of the fourth day, Miss James put a fresh bandage on his leg. Right afterward he went to see Peter, the little boy, who lived next door.

The bandage was tied in a neat bow. The bow came quite high up on Buzzie's leg. As he hobbled along on three legs, the bow bobbed up and down. It looked very nice against his gray fur.

Peter was playing in the wide driveway near his house.

"Hello, Buzzie," he said, and patted Buzzie's head. Then he said, "Oh, what's the matter with your paw?"

"It got stuck in a tin can. A very tough tin can. I had to stay in the woods all night," Buzzie said.

He rubbed up against Peter's legs and began to purr. He was so happy to have someone to talk to.

"Weren't you afraid?" Peter asked.

"Who? Me?" Buzzie asked. "Why, there were wolves and bears in the woods where I was. They came out at night and I chased 'em away."

"My! But you're brave!" Peter said.

"Well, of course it did get a little lonely," Buzzie said. "And I really wasn't in the woods. I was in some deep high grass."

46

He remembered the dog smell and the skunk smell and the memory made him shiver. "To tell you the truth I *was* scared. I didn't know whether I'd ever get home."

Buzzie purred very loudly after he said this. He was pleased to find that he sounded much braver because he said that he'd been afraid.

He added, "There really weren't any wolves and bears. I made up that part. But a dog did go by and a skunk walked past, and they scared me."

He walked up and down the driveway, hip-hopping on his three good legs. He glanced at Peter out of the corners of his eyes. "I think the lions and tigers were the worst part," he said.

Peter sat right down in the middle of the driveway and laughed and laughed. "Go on!" he said. "I don't believe you."

Buzzie's short tail started switching back and forth, back and forth, the way it did when he was angry. He hip-hopped across the driveway, holding his bandaged paw high off the ground.

47

As he crawled under the picket fence he muttered to himself, "Of course there weren't any lions and tigers in the meadow. I was going to tell Peter a fairy tale. And it's rude to tell a cat you don't believe him when he's going to tell you a fairy tale."

He was so angry that he did not take an afternoon nap. Instead he sat down on the store steps, right in front of the screen door. He kept blinking his eyes and switching his tail back and forth, as he stared at the road and at the big elm trees across the street.

He said, "DRUMSTICKS!" twice, softly.

The sun was shining on the steps. It was warm there. Finally, he dozed a little.

He was half-asleep when a yellow roadster pulled up in front of the store. A young woman got out of the car. She quickly crossed the dirt path, and hurried up the steps. Then she paused with her hand on the screen door.

Buzzie did not move.

"Come on, Cat," the young woman said, "Move out of the way."

She could have opened the screen door and stepped over Buzzie, and gone inside. But she was angry, too. And as she waited for him to move, she started tapping her foot on the step.

"Move out of the way yourself!" Buzzie answered angrily. His short tail moved back and forth, back and forth, faster than before. He stood up and hissed at her, "H-ssttt!"

"You're a short-tempered little cat!" the young woman said. "Your temper is just as short as your tail. I'm not going to stand here in the sun, on a hot afternoon like this and let any little bob-tail cat hiss at me!"

"A bob-tail cat!" Buzzie said. "A bob-tail cat! I'm no bob-tail cat. I'll have you know my father was a Manx cat. And I take after him."

The young woman did not understand a single word that Buzzie said. Leaning over, she started to push him out of the way.

Buzzie was so angry that he gave a little jump and slapped at her with his unbandaged paw. He hit the

49

palm of her outstretched hand with his claws.

"Ouch!" the young woman said. "Miss James! Miss James! Your little cat scratched me."

"What?" Miss James said, opening the screen door. She came outside and stood on the steps.

"Your little cat scratched me," the young woman said and held her hand out for Miss James to see.

"Come inside and I'll wash it off," Miss James said.

Buzzie watched them go in the store. "I don't care!" he said to himself. "That girl had no right to try to push me in the first place." Then he said, softly, "I guess my temper *is* pretty short, though," and he sighed.

When the young woman came out of the store, Buzzie went inside. He hopped across the linoleum floor and sat down in front of Miss James.

Miss James was talking to her brother. "I hate to send Buzzie away," she said.

"Send me away?" Buzzie said. He couldn't believe his ears. This was his new home. He belonged

here in the drugstore. Miss James couldn't mean to send him away, right out of his own house.

"It's a good thing I'm not the kind of cat that goes in for crying," he said, under his breath.

Miss James went right on talking to her brother. "Buzzie just scratched Mary Butler. And Mary said that we've got to get rid of him or she won't come in the drugstore any more. She spends so much money with us that I'll have to do as she says."

Miss James looked down at Buzzie over the top of her glasses. She shook her head. "He's such a nice little cat. I hate to send him back to his mother. But there's nothing else to do. As soon as his paw is well, you'll have to take him back to the barn where you got him."

"Oh, please don't do that!" Buzzie said. He had missed his home in the barn, and his brothers and sisters, and his mother. He had wanted to go back there. But not like this. What in the world would his mother say!

Miss James and her brother went right on talking

as though Buzzie had not spoken. Finally, Miss James said to her brother, "You know sometimes Buzzie acts as though he could talk."

Buzzie looked at them both, very sadly. "I can talk," he said. "But not everybody can understand me."

CHAPTER SIX

Buzzie Tries To Lengthen His Temper

The next morning, right after breakfast, Buzzie went to see Peter, the little boy who lived next door to the drugstore. He crossed the wide driveway, walking very fast, on his three good legs. The bow on his bandaged leg kept bobbing up and down, up and down.

Outside the kitchen door of Peter's house, he said, "Meow," very softly.

Buzzie Tries To Lengthen His Temper

Peter came to the door. "Hello, Buzzie," he said. "Wait a minute. I'll be right out."

Buzzie sat down on the kitchen steps. Then in a few minutes Peter came outside and sat down beside him.

"Say, what was the matter with you yesterday?" Peter asked.

"I was angry," Buzzie said. He turned his head and looked at his short tail. "My temper seems to be as short as my tail. But beginning today I'm going to lengthen my temper out. Then perhaps Miss James won't send me back to my mother. I'd be a very polite cat if I had a long temper."

"Is Miss James going to send you back?" Peter asked.

"Yes. I scratched a girl yesterday. And Miss James says I've got to go back to the barn as soon as my paw is well," Buzzie said sadly.

"Can't you get her to change her mind?"

"No," Buzzie said. "Her mind is made up. Whenever her mind is made up she looks over the

55

top of her glasses. And she's been looking over the top of her glasses ever since yesterday."

All of a sudden, Buzzie sat up very straight. "Say," he said, "do you think maybe I could live at your house?"

Peter shook his head. "No," he said. "My mother doesn't like cats. And she told me she especially doesn't like short-tailed little cats."

"Short-tailed little cats! Short-tailed—" Buzzie sputtered, angrily. He jumped down from the steps and had hip-hopped halfway across the wide driveway before he remembered that he was supposed to be lengthening his temper out.

He stood still. Then he looked very ashamed. He walked slowly toward the steps. Sitting down beside Peter, he blinked his eyes.

"At this rate I'll never be able to lengthen my temper out—" he said. But he didn't finish the rest of what he was going to say because just then Mr. Smith walked by.

When Mr. Smith saw Peter and Buzzie sitting on

the steps, he stopped and leaned against the picket fence. He lifted his wide-brimmed hat and said, "Good morning to you both! This is a rare and lovely morning. Especially good for all growing things—small boys and young cats and the new grass that grows so smooth and green. A rare and lovely morning!"

Peter and Buzzie got up from the steps and started running toward the fence. For as Mr. Smith stood there, leaning against the fence, he twirled his gold-headed cane, and it glowed in the sunlight.

Buzzie kept getting closer and closer to Mr. Smith. Finally, he sat right down on one of Mr. Smith's white shoes. Mr. Smith began to swing his big foot back and forth, back and forth, oh, so gently!

"Look at me! Look at me!" Buzzie cried. "I'm going for a ride. Look at me go!"

"It's a shoe swing, Buzzie. You're in a shoe swing," Peter said, laughing. "Hold on tight!"

While Buzzie sat swinging back and forth on Mr.

57

Smith's foot, he told Mr. Smith that Miss James was going to send him home. "And I'm trying to lengthen my temper out so that she'll want to keep me. But it's very hard to do," he said and sighed.

"Mmmm," said Mr. Smith, thoughtfully. "Like everything else there's a trick to it. It's not too hard and, on the other hand, it's not too easy."

Mr. Smith twirled his cane for a moment, around and around, and the gold head spun so fast and shone so much that it looked like a little running sun.

"I know!" said Mr. Smith. "Whenever you get angry, before you say a word, or do a single thing, you count up to ten. Now you listen with both ears, and with your eyes, too. Because that's the best kind of listening there is. This is what you say:

"One mouse	Five mice
Two mice	Six mice
Three mice	Seven mice
Four mice	Eight mice

Nine mice

TEN mice!"

Mr. Smith sounded as though he were singing when he said this. "By the time you count as far as 'TEN mice' you'll be feeling very polite and your temper will be so long it will reach to the top of that great big elm tree."

Peter and Buzzie and Mr. Smith started counting together, "One mouse, Two mice—"

Buzzie swayed back and forth on Mr. Smith's foot as they counted. And it was very much like sitting in a rocking chair and being sung to.

While Buzzie sat there on Mr. Smith's foot, lengthening his temper seemed very easy. But he found it wasn't quite so easy as that. Sometimes he had to count as far as ' TEN mice' before he could be polite.

CHAPTER SEVEN

Buzzie's Temper Grows Long

Whenever Mr. Smith went for his morning walk, he always stopped at the drugstore to give Buzzie a ride on his shoe. And each and every morning Mr. Smith said, "Why, I can fairly see your temper growing longer and longer!"

It was true, too. Buzzie rarely ever lost his temper any more.

He wanted to be certain that Miss James saw how

61

polite he had become so he never let her get out of his sight for very long. When she opened the store in the morning, he came downstairs right in back of her. He hobbled along on his three good legs, holding his hurt paw high up off the stairs.

After she opened the big front door, he sat down in the doorway, sniffing the fresh morning air. He spoke politely to all of the people who came in the store.

The customers patted his head and stroked his soft gray fur. He no longer walked away from them. Instead he purred so loudly he sounded like a small motor—buzz-zz, buzz-zz, buzz-zz.

Though he talked to all the people who came into the store, none of them understood what he said. Sometimes he wondered why Mr. Smith, who was very, very old, and Peter, who was very, very young, could understand him. But he was so busy lengthening out his temper that he didn't have much time to think about it.

During the day he took his naps in the big front

window of the store. Mr. James had put a small basket in there for him. Quite often someone going past would see Buzzie, sleeping in the basket. A man or a woman would stop and tap on the glass and wake him up.

At first Buzzie had to count up as far as 'TEN mice' before he could be polite. Finally, he only had to begin to count, "One mouse, Two mice—"

Then he would get out of the basket and walk up and down in the big window, purring very loudly, showing how friendly he was.

He kept hoping that Miss James would change her mind about sending him back to his mother. Whenever she sat down he jumped up in her lap and began to purr, very loudly, looking up at her, and blinking his eyes.

He followed her all around the store, walking right behind her. If she unpacked a box in the small back room, he would get inside the box. Then you could see only the top of his small gray head, peering out. When she reached inside the box to take out a package, he touched her hand with one of his soft paws, to show her how gently he could play.

Sometimes she opened the candy case and gave him a very small piece of chocolate. He purred and purred as he licked the chocolate. After that, whenever he went behind the candy counter he always poked at the door of the case, on the chance that Miss James might have left it open.

One morning he found out just how long his temper had grown.

A very, very fat lady came in the drugstore. She had on a long, full gingham dress. The skirt came down to her ankles. As the fat lady walked around the store, Buzzie walked right behind her.

The flip of her long full skirt was like the flutter of a bird's wing.

Buzzie followed the fat lady's skirt, crouching down and taking little running steps toward it, getting closer and closer. He poked at the hem of the skirt with his paw. He almost caught the edge of the billowy material.

64

Suddenly the fat lady stood still. Buzzie gave a little pounce and he caught hold of the hem of the long full skirt. His claws fastened in the material.

"Mercy me!" cried the fat lady, startled. She looked around and saw Buzzie clinging to the hem of her skirt. She gave a very fat jump.

She tried to move away from him. He moved with her. All four of his feet came up off the floor as the big gingham skirt swirled around.

The fat lady's face turned red. "Skat!" she cried. "Skat!" She gave her skirt a hard shake. Buzzie landed on the floor, so hard and so fast that he lost his breath.

He was very angry. His short tail swelled in size. "The nerve of you!" he muttered. "Saying 'Skat!' to me!"

He took a deep breath, for he was getting ready to say, "DRUMSTICKS!" in his very loudest, angriest voice.

Then he remembered that he was lengthening his temper. He swallowed his breath and his favorite word all at the same time. He gulped as they went down, for 'drumsticks' is a long word to swallow.

He began to count, "One mouse, Two mice, Three mice—"

When he got as far as Three mice, his breath came out in a small sigh. He said, "Mee-ouch!" in a little gentle voice, just to show his feelings were hurt.

The fat lady leaned way over and her fat full skirt spread way out. She patted Buzzie's head and said, "Oh, I'm so sorry. Did I hurt you?"

As the fat lady stroked his head, Buzzie began to purr. The soft murmur of the fat lady's voice was as lovely as the velvety sound of his mother's purring.

After the fat lady went out of the store, Buzzie said to himself, "Why, I actually have a long temper!"

He was almost certain Miss James would keep him now. He had certainly shown her how polite he had grown. For the rest of the day he walked about, very proudly, holding his short tail straight up in the air and purring to himself.

CHAPTER EIGHT

Buzzie Meets the Ice Cream Man

The next morning, Buzzie was still so proud of himself that he didn't take his usual morning nap. Instead, he went to see his friend Peter, the little boy who lived next door.

He told Peter all about the fat lady and how she had said "Scat!" to him, and how polite he had been about it.

They were sitting on the steps of Peter's house.

Buzzie Meets the Ice Cream Man

All of a sudden, Peter said, "Oh, here comes the ice cream man!"

He jumped up so quickly that he almost stepped on Buzzie. He ran toward the picket fence. Buzzie ran after him, hopping along on three legs, going just as fast as he could.

Peter opened the gate, ran across the lawn and toward the road in front of the drugstore. A big red truck was parked there. And across the side of the truck in yellow letters were the words: ICE CREAM.

The ice cream man was standing by the truck. He was a big jolly fellow. He had very blue eyes and very red cheeks. He was always whistling and always laughing.

Quite often when he was pulling the big cans of ice cream out of the truck he sang a song. It went like this:

> I sell ice cream,
> Chocolate, Cherry,
> It makes folks dream,
> It keeps 'em merry!

69

The Drugstore Cat

When the ice cream man saw Buzzie and Peter running toward him, he threw back his head and laughed so hard he very nearly cried. He said, "Look at that little cat run! Look at that little boy run!"

His blue eyes twinkled and he couldn't talk for laughing. His laughter was the merriest sound you've ever heard.

He opened the back door of the big red truck. Then he picked up a shiny scoop. The scoop shone like silver in the sunlight. He scooped out some ice cream and put it in a paper cup and placed the cup on the path in front of Buzzie. Then he scooped out some ice cream and put it in a paper dish and handed it to Peter.

Buzzie had never eaten any ice cream before. He began to purr the instant he tasted it, and he didn't stop purring until he had licked the little paper cup clean.

He watched the ice cream man take big cans out of the back of the red truck and carry them into the drugstore.

"Say," Buzzie said. "I've never seen him before."

"That's because you sleep so much," Peter said. "You're always taking a nap when he comes."

"If I'm asleep the next time he comes, you call me. I wouldn't ever want to miss him again," Buzzie said. He licked the little paper dish again to make certain he hadn't left any ice cream around the edges of it.

Sitting in the middle of the path, he washed his face and cleaned his whiskers. While he was giving his whiskers a final polish he hoped, more than ever, that Miss James had changed her mind about sending him home to his mother.

After that Buzzie sat in the path, every morning, waiting for the ice cream truck. Sometimes Peter was with him, and sometimes he wasn't.

But Peter never had to call Buzzie to tell him that the big red truck was in front of the drugstore.

Whenever Buzzie was by himself the ice cream man would pretend he didn't see the small, fat, kitten sitting in the middle of the path. Just for the fun of it, the ice cream man would glance all around, at the big elm trees, across the street at the church steeple which went up and up, at the green hedge in front of the drugstore. He even looked into the wide front window of the store.

Opening the screen door of the drugstore, he called out, "*Is* there, in this drugstore, a very small cat who wants some ice cream, ICE CREAM, ICE CREAM?"

Finally he looked down at his feet. By this time, Buzzie was walking in between his legs, in and out, in and out, talking away at a great rate.

The ice cream man couldn't understand a word Buzzie said but he laughed his merry laugh. He said, "Ho-ho! There's that little Buzzie cat. How about some ice cream on this fine summer morning?"

When he gave Buzzie some ice cream, Buzzie purred so loudly that his small sides shook.

With each passing day Buzzie's paw got better and better. By the time he could step on it without saying, "Mee-ouch!" he had forgotten he ever wished to be back in the barn. He was the most polite little cat you have ever seen! He no longer had to count even as far as 'Three mice' in order to keep his temper.

He was certain Miss James had changed her mind about sending him back to his mother. And he was very happy for he loved the drugstore and Miss James and her brother, Mr. James.

He liked sleeping on the red cushion in the kitchen, and playing in the big backyard where the grass grew so smooth and green.

By this time he had so many friends that he was never lonesome. There was Peter, the little boy who lived next door; and old Mr. Smith, who gave him a ride on his shoe each and every morning; and the big jolly ice cream man who whistled and sang while he dipped out ice cream with a scoop that shone like silver in the sunlight.

And then, one morning, Miss James looked over the top of her glasses at Buzzie. He was chasing his short tail, around and around. He skipped about on all four legs, just as though his right paw had never been hurt.

Miss James said to her brother, "I'll have to send Buzzie back to his mother tomorrow. His paw is well."

Buzzie stopped chasing his tail. "*Please* don't do that," he said.

Miss James did not answer him.

"Oh," said Buzzie. "I wish, I wish, OH, how I wish I could stay here in the drugstore."

Miss James and her brother could not understand a word he said. But they were so upset at the thought of sending Buzzie back to his mother that when they closed the drugstore for the night they forgot to lock the big front door.

CHAPTER NINE

Buzzie Saves the Drugstore

That night, as usual, Buzzie slept on the red cushion in Miss James's kitchen. He did not sleep very well. He kept waking up and looking around him, for fear he had been taken back to his old home in the barn while he was asleep. His nose twitched and he moved his paws as though he were running.

Toward midnight, someone walked around the side of the building, tried one of the kitchen windows.

Buzzie Saves the Drugstore

The sound awakened Buzzie. He opened his eyes wide. They glowed like small lanterns in the dark. He sat up, listening. There was a hasty movement outside the kitchen window and then the footsteps went away.

"I wonder what that was," Buzzie said to himself.

He walked all around the kitchen, and then he padded softly up the stairs. He went into Miss James's bedroom. She was sound asleep and breathing very softly, very evenly.

Walking slowly and sedately, he went down the hall and peered into Mr. James's bedroom. Mr. James was snoring. He was making a noise like a big bumblebee.

"Should think he'd wake himself up," Buzzie said.

While he was standing in the doorway of Mr. James's room he heard a clicking sound. It sounded like the opening of the latch on the big front door of the drugstore.

He walked toward the staircase which led down

into the drugstore. He crouched down at the top of the stairs, listening.

Someone was moving around in the store. There were quiet footsteps and then the sound of a case being opened.

"Maybe that's the ice cream man," Buzzie said.

He ran down the steps so fast that he fell on the bottom step.

"Mmm, kind of missed my step," he said.

He hurried through the little backroom and then into the main part of the drugstore. Two men were standing behind the candy counter. Buzzie did not even look at them. The rich, thick smell of chocolate was in his nose and he sniffed the air, delicately. He went behind the counter, lifted one paw and poked at the door of the candy case to see if Miss James had left it open.

A man's foot landed heavily on Buzzie's paw.

"Mee-ouch!" cried Buzzie. "Get off my foot! Why don't you look where you're going?"

"What's that?" the man said, startled. He directed

the beam from his flashlight down toward his feet.

The sudden brilliant light surprised Buzzie, and made him angrier, too. He hissed, "S-s-tt!"

He was much too angry to be polite. His fur was very fat-looking, every hair stood up by itself. Even his short tail had swelled in size. His eyes looked enormous and very yellow.

"Go away!" The man shouted and jumped back, away from Buzzie. For Buzzie was practically under his feet, hissing and snarling.

The man's elbow went through the glass of the wall case behind him. The glass crashed in with a loud, splintering sound.

"Now look what you've done!" said the other man. "We've got to get out of here. Quick!"

The men started for the door, moving so fast that they bumped into each other. Then they ran out of the drugstore.

There was the sound of hurried footsteps on the stairs. Buzzie blinked his eyes, trying to get used to the darkness after the sudden shaft of light.

Listening to the steps on the stairs, he said, "Must be Mr. James. He sure walks hard."

Buzzie was standing in the doorway of the store, looking out at the quiet street, when Mr. James turned on the store lights. Mr. James walked all around the store, looking at the shelves, opening the show cases. Buzzie walked right in back of him.

Mr. James leaned over and patted Buzzie's head. "I don't think they stole anything," he said. He was talking to himself and he walked over and looked at the big front door. "Why it wasn't even locked!" he said. "I wonder how those robbers broke the glass in that case. That's what woke me up."

"There were two of them. One of them stepped on my foot," said Buzzie. "I got mad and made a lot of noise. And the man jumped back. His elbow went through the case and broke the glass."

Buzzie sat down and lifted the paw that had been stepped on. He was getting ready to wash it.

And then it happened. Mr. James said politely, "What did you say?"

Buzzie kept his paw in the same position, halfway to his mouth.

He stared at Mr. James. Then he told him, again, how the man had stepped on his paw, and then backed into the glass case, breaking it with his elbow.

Mr. James said, "Well, that certainly was the right time to be angry. You saved the drugstore!"

Buzzie got up and started walking in and out, in and out, between Mr. James's long legs. "This is very queer," he said. "How is it you can understand cat language now when you never could before?"

Mr. James did not answer.

At that very moment, Miss James came running into the drugstore. She was breathing very hard. Her gray hair hung down in two long braids and the braids were moving about as though they were excited, too. She had on a white nightgown and a blue dressing gown. And she was hurrying so fast that the hem of the long white nightgown looked as though it were running–all by itself.

"Oh, what happened? What happened?" she said

to her brother, Mr. James. "What was that noise?"

"I ran the robbers away," Buzzie said.

But Miss James did not answer him.

"Now don't get excited," Mr. James said to his sister. "Buzzie saved us from being robbed. We left the front door open last night and two robbers walked right in. One of the men stepped on Buzzie's paw. Buzzie made so much noise that the man was frightened and backed into a showcase and broke it. They ran out of the store so fast they didn't have time to steal anything."

Miss James looked frightened. Then she looked pleased. "Oh, how wonderful!" she said. "Buzzie is the smartest little cat!" Looking hard at Mr. James she said, "How did you know one of the men stepped on Buzzie's foot?"

Mr. James frowned. "Why–" he said and stopped talking. He sighed and rubbed the side of his face. "I'm not quite sure–Isn't that funny–I think Buzzie told me."

Miss James looked at Mr. James over the top of

her glasses. "Now, really–" she said. "Now really!"

Buzzie walked over to Miss James. He sat down just under the edge of the long, white nightgown. You could see only the top of his small gray head. And in his very best speaking voice he said, "*Please* don't send me back to my mother!"

Miss James leaned down and picked Buzzie up. She patted the top of his head, stroked his soft gray fur.

"I don't care whether Mary Butler comes in the store again or not," she said to her brother. "I'm not going to send Buzzie away. This is his home. He's going to stay here. He's earned the right to stay here."

Buzzie purred very loudly. Then he said, between purrs, "When I first came to the drugstore to live I didn't think I'd like it. Now I wouldn't want to live any other place!"

Miss James did not answer. Buzzie looked at Mr. James. "Why can't she understand what I say?" he asked.

84

Mr. James did not answer either. Buzzie wriggled out of Miss James's arms. He sat down in the middle of the floor and began to wash his face, all over, very carefully. Now and then he looked up at Miss James and then at her brother.

"Sometimes when I look at Buzzie and he looks at me I get the feeling that he's talking to me," Miss James said.

Mr. James tightened the sash of his dressing gown. "He does talk," he said.

And when his sister stared hard at him over the top of her glasses, Mr. James started turning out the lights in the drugstore.

Just before they went out of the store, Buzzie heard Mr. James say, "I heard Buzzie talk tonight—just for a little while. And I'm pretty certain that one of these days I'll be able to understand every word he says."

Long after Mr. James had turned the lights out, Buzzie sat in the drugstore.

"Sometime soon," he said to himself. "I shall go

85

and visit my mother. She'll be very proud of me when I tell her how I scared the robbers away."

He got up and padded softly all around the store, talking to himself as he went. "This is a very good place to live. A very, very good place," he said. He sniffed at the edge of the candy case and poked at the door just to make certain that it hadn't somehow been left open since the last time he tried it.

Suddenly he stood still. "I wonder why Mr. James heard what I said tonight when he never did before. And I wonder why Peter and old Mr. Smith can always understand me," he said, thoughtfully.

He thought about this so hard and so fast that he had to stop thinking and chase his tail for a few minutes, in order to give himself time to catch up with his thoughts.

He went around, and around. He never did catch his tail, after all it was very short, and very hard to catch, but he did catch up with his thoughts.

When he caught up with his thoughts, he said, softly, under his breath, "I know what it is! I know what it is! Very, very young people and very, very old people understand everything better than anyone else. That's why Peter and Mr. Smith can understand cat language."

Then his thoughts started going so fast that he had to blink his eyes and take a deep breath, in order to hold onto them.

When his thoughts had slowed down a little, he said, "Pretty soon Mr. James will be able to understand every word I say. He's right on the tip edge of getting old. That's why he understood me tonight— for a little while. And one of these days Miss James will understand cat language, too."

After he said this he sat down, right in the middle of the drugstore. He began to purr, for he was very happy.

As he sat there he purred louder and louder. And he sounded exactly like a small, warm-motor— buzz-zz, buzz-zz, buzz-zz.